Library of Congress Cataloging-in-Publication Data Available

KOHL'S
ISBN 978-1-4549-1386-3
Factory Number: 131076
4/14

Distributed in Canada by Sterling Publishing
c/o Canadian Manda Group, 165 Dufferin Street
Toronto, Ontario, Canada M6K 3H6
Distributed in the United Kingdom by GMC Distribution Services
Castle Place, 166 High Street, Lewes, East Sussex, England BN7 1XU
Distributed in Australia by Capricorn Link (Australia) Pty. Ltd.
P.O. Box 704, Windsor, NSW 2756, Australia

A Big Tuna New Media LLC/ J.R. Sansevere Book

For information about custom editions, special sales, and premium and corporate purchases,
please contact Sterling Special Sales at 800-805-5489 or specialsales@sterlingpublishing.com.

This special edition was printed for Kohl's Department Stores, Inc. (for distribution on behalf of Kohl's Cares,
LLC, its wholly owned subsidiary) by Sterling Publishing.

Manufactured in China
Lot #:
2 4 6 8 10 9 7 5 3 1
04/14

www.sterlingpublishing.com/kids

LITTLE CRITTER®
HANSEL AND GRETEL

a lift-the-flap
book

by MERCER MAYER

STERLING CHILDREN'S BOOKS
New York

One day Hansel and Gretel took a walk in the woods. They went so far that they got lost.
A little bird warned them to turn back, but they paid him no mind.

They found a wonderful
gingerbread house all covered
with icing and candy.
They were very hungry so
Gretel rang the doorbell.

An old witch lived there. She pretended to be a sweet, little old lady.

She invited them inside and offered them good things to eat. But the food was enchanted and made them sleepy.

The old witch gave them soft
feather beds to sleep on. Then late
that night she crept in, grabbed Hansel,
and stuffed him into a sack.

She put Hansel down in the dungeon and made Gretel bring food to him every day.
The old witch wanted to fatten him up to make a critter pie out of him.

All she gave Gretel to eat were a few scraps from her table and some breadcrumbs.

The old witch made Gretel sweep
and clean. And while she worked,
the old witch took a nap.
That didn't make Gretel very happy.

WHAT'S GOING TO
HAPPEN NEXT?

"Fetch me some water from the well,"
said the old witch one day.
Gretel went outside and called,
"Dear old witch, I have dropped the
bucket in the well and I'm too little
to reach it. Please help me!"

The old witch grumbled, but she
went outside.

She didn't see Gretel anywhere.
The old witch leaned over the well
to reach the bucket.